HANDS UP!

by **Breanna J. McDaniel** • illustrated by **Shane W. Evans**

PUFFIN BOOKS

Greet the sun, bold and bright!

Tiny hands up!

Peek-a-boo—
hands up!

"Morning, baby.
Time to get dressed, hands up."

Stretch high!
Almost there, **hands up.**

Gotta get clean.
Reach for the sink, hands up.

"C'mon, little one, dry your tears.
Here, hold the bun, hands up."

Ready for takeoff, hands up!

"Please pick me, Ms. B!
Got my hands up!"

Adventure books live up top.
Reach high, tippy toes, hands up!

Graceful like Ms. Misty.
Fifth position, **hands up.**

Racing fast,
wind whistling,
hands up . . .

"It's all right, baby girl,
I'll help, hands up."

The music flows through us.
"Aaaa-may-zi-in' grace!"
In praise and worship, hands up!

On the court fired up, jump ball, hands up . . .

"For the win, defense, hands up!"

On top of the world,
trophy to the sky, **hands up!**

We begin small, but we grow big.
Together we are mighty.
High fives all around, **hands up!**

SPREAD LOVE
NINGÚN
HUMANO
ES ILEGAL
WATER
=LIFE
OVE YOUR
NEIGHBO

As one we say, "HANDS UP!"

Notes from the Author and Artist

Dear Friends,

My niece Taylor's smile is warm like the Georgia sun in July. She's mischievous and snuggly; she's eager to explore new things, but she knows her momma's warmth is nearby if new starts to feel scary. She's cheerful and clever and sometimes stubborn. She's awesome!

Sometimes, I worry that this world is not a place where Taylor can show all her joy, her intelligence and the strength of her will without being seen as a social problem, all because she's Black and a girl. I worry that this world casts Black kids as victims, villains, or simply adults before they're grown up. And because of that, sometimes they don't get a chance to grow up at all.

For many people, the phrase "hands up" brings forward difficult emotions like anger, sadness, frustration, and fear. With this story, I wanted to emphasize the ways I've experienced that phrase as part of my everyday life: at home, at play, in church, and at protests with young people leading the way. I want the world to remember that Black kids are just that—kids, people with mommas and daddies and teachers and friends, with lives full of happiness and struggle and triumph and even sadness.

Kids, I know you see and understand far more than a lot of us adults think you do. This book is my chance to tell you just how important your voices and lives are. Your health and happiness, your agency and humanity make our world whole.

You matter. Your joy will be celebrated. Your struggles will be supported. Your love will be returned. You deserve to thrive.

Love and Light,

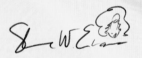

While working on this book, I realized every line and color was an important mark toward raising the hands of people throughout the world. I pray we have not forgotten the basics, but I see that we are constantly looking down when we should be looking up. We should be putting our hands up high to show how bright and full we truly are. As an illustrator, I often act out the story to learn how to draw it. This brilliant reminder from Breanna helped guide me back to lifting my hands in joy. I stopped being afraid of raising my hands up, and stretching them high felt right. It felt good to celebrate. So, to you all: Celebrate with me. HANDS UP!

Dear Momma, Bethani, and Trish:
This first one is for you.
—B.J.M.

Thank God for the gift. I dedicate this book to my family and agape love . . . the love that covers us all.
—S.W.E.

PUFFIN BOOKS • An imprint of Penguin Random House LLC, New York

First published in the United States of America by Dial Books for Young Readers, 2019
Published by Puffin Books, an imprint of Penguin Random House LLC, 2020

THE LIBRARY OF CONGRESS HAS CATALOGED THE DIAL EDITION AS FOLLOWS:
Names: McDaniel, Breanna J., author. | Evans, Shane, illustrator. Title: Hands up! / Breanna J. McDaniel ; illustrated by Shane W. Evans.
Description: New York, NY : Dial Books for Young Readers, [2019] | Summary: "A young girl lifts her hands up in a series of everyday moments before finally raising her hands in resistance at a protest march" —Provided by publisher.
Identifiers: LCCN 2018015398 | ISBN 9780525552314 (hardcover) Subjects: | CYAC: Family life—Fiction. | African Americans—Fiction. Classification: LCC PZ7.1.M43432 Han 2019 | DDC [E]—dc23 LC record available at https://lccn.loc.gov/2018015398

Manufactured in China • Puffin Books ISBN 9780593326640 • 10 9 8 7 6 5 4 3 2 1

Design by Jasmin Rubero • Text set in Buenos Aires Trail

The art for this book is created digitally with mixed media.